STAR WARS™

THE CLONE WARS™

THE HUNT FOR GRIEVOUS

adapted by Christopher Cerasi

based on the TV series STAR WARS: THE CLONE WARS

After a daring assault on a Jedi cruiser, the evil cyborg leader of the Separatist droid army, General Grievous, succeeded in capturing his prey, Jedi Master Eeth Koth.

The Jedi Council learned that Grievous was taking Master Koth to the planet Saleucami.

Obi-Wan Kenobi, Anakin Skywalker and Jedi Master Adi Gallia were ordered to stop Grievous and rescue the Jedi Master.

As the Jedi were leaving Coruscant, Adi Gallia said "If Master Koth is still alive, we will find him."

Obi-Wan agreed.

"Hopefully by the end of this mission," he said, "we will have saved Master Koth *and* captured General Grievous."

Obi-Wan and Commander Cody left in a small cruiser to divert Grievous's attention.

Anakin and Adi Gallia planned to sneak on board the general's ship – while he was distracted with Captain Rex and a group of clone troopers – and rescue Eeth Koth.

High above the planet Saleucami, General Grievous ordered his droids to begin landing and setting up a base.

Behind the general on the bridge of his ship was the injured Eeth Koth.

Just then, several ships came out of hyperspace in front of Grievous's vessel. The general quickly realized they were Republic ships.

Grievous turned to Eeth Koth and laughed. "You see, your compassionate friends have come to rescue you, just as I knew they would."

An image of Obi-Wan Kenobi appeared on the ship's viewscreen. Grievous narrowed his eyes at the sight of the Jedi.

"Kenobi! What a surprise," he said. "I assume you are here to bring me to justice?"

"You know me too well," replied Obi-Wan.

"Indeed I do!" Grievous then turned to his droids. "Prepare to fire all

cannons, and be alert. Where there is Kenobi, you will always find Skywalker not far behind."

The general pointed to Obi-Wan's ship. "I want to board that vessel."

Obi-Wan made sure the Republic ships kept General Grievous occupied so that Anakin and Adi Gallia could arrive undetected.

The Jedi Master waited with Commander Cody on the bridge of his small cruiser. After a few seconds, he had the coordinates of Grievous's ship. Anakin and Adi Gallia sent the information back to the Jedi Council on Coruscant.

Anakin plotted his course to meet Obi-Wan and then launched his ship into hyperspace.

Back near Saleucami, General Grievous activated his ship's tractor beam and pulled Obi-Wan's cruiser towards his vessel.

A docking tube appeared from the side of Grievous's ship and attached to Obi-Wan's ship, connecting the two.

Obi-Wan led Commander Cody and the other clone troopers down a corridor and waited for Grievous to enter.

Obi-Wan turned to his men. "Remember, we need to keep Grievous on this ship until General Skywalker is clear."

A team of commando droids forced their way aboard the Republic ship and quickly engaged the clone troopers.

Grievous and his MagnaGuards pushed their way through towards Obi-Wan. MagnaGuards surrounded the Jedi as Grievous stepped forward.

"So, Kenobi," Grievous asked, "is everything going as planned?"

Obi-Wan quickly cut down two MagnaGuards with his lightsaber. "That depends on your point of view, General," he said.

"You wouldn't come here without a plan," Grievous wheezed. "And you wouldn't come here alone. Tell me, do you think Skywalker has rescued Master Koth yet?"

Obi-Wan realized that General Grievous was on to his plan and hoped that Anakin would be safe.

Meanwhile, Anakin's shuttle secretly emerged from hyperspace. Carefully, he attached the shuttle to the hull of Grievous's ship and cut his way in with his lightsaber. Anakin, Adi Gallia, Rex and several clones, climbed up through the hole and into a deserted corridor.

Anakin turned to Rex and his men. "Stay here and guard the entrance. This may be our only way out."

As Rex nodded, Adi looked at her wrist-communicator. "Master Koth is located on the bridge. This way," she said.

A few minutes later, they found Eeth Koth on the bridge. He didn't look too good and needed medical help. As Anakin and Adi Gallia went to free their

friend, they were quickly surrounded by a dozen commando droids.

The two Jedi rushed to release Eeth Koth from the energy shackles. He was weak and they had to help him stand up.

"Where's General Grievous?" he asked.

"If everything has gone according to plan, he's on board Obi-Wan's ship," Anakin replied.

"Has he been captured?" Eeth Koth asked.

"If we cut off his escape," Anakin said, "there's a good chance he is! Master Gallia, you go ahead and help Obi-Wan. I'll get Master Koth back to the shuttle."

As Adi Gallia prepared to leave, she looked at Anakin and Eeth Koth with a brave face. "May the Force be with you," she said, then turned and ran.

Back on Obi-Wan's ship, the Jedi battled with General Grievous and the remaining MagnaGuard.

"Your plans have come to ruination, Jedi!" said Grievous, trying to confuse Obi-Wan.

Obi-Wan battled the MagnaGuard as Grievous watched.

"I hear a lot of talking," Obi-Wan said. "But in the final accounting, what does all the talk get you?"

"I'm no errand boy . . . And I'm not in the war for Dooku's politics,"

Grievous replied. "I'm the leader of the most powerful droid army this galaxy has ever seen!"

"An army with no loyalty . . . No spirit. Just programming. What have you to show for all your power?" Obi-Wan asked. "What have you to gain?"

"The future," Grievous answered as he extended all four of his arms and advanced on Obi-Wan. "A future where there are no Jedi!"

Obi-Wan tried to fight back, but Grievous sent him flying. Grievous moved towards Obi-Wan, his lightsabers ready.

"The story of Obi-Wan Kenobi ends here!" Grievous crowed.

Obi-Wan quickly got back on his feet and moved towards General Grievous.

"Surrender, General," he said, pointing his lightsaber at the general.

"Never!" Grievous cried as he leaped past Obi-Wan and scuttled towards the tube connecting the two ships.

But his path was blocked by Cody and his clone troopers.

Grievous continued to move towards the tube, swinging his lightsabers at the clone troopers. Several clones fell, but Cody was determined to keep Grievous on board the Jedi's ship.

Obi-Wan rounded the corner and found two clones heading towards him.

"Get back to the bridge," he called out. "We need to detach before Grievous jumps ship!"

As Grievous entered the docking tube, he called the droids on his ship with his wrist comlink.

"Open fire on the Republic ship," he ordered. "Target their engines. It doesn't matter that we are still attached. Prepare all troops for our landing on Saleucami!"

Grievous looked behind him and saw that Obi-Wan, Cody, and a few clone troopers had entered the docking tube. The tube began to shake as blaster bolts from Grievous's ship hit the Republic cruiser.

Aboard the cruiser, the two clone pilots were trying to hold the ship together "We have no controls," one of the pilots announced. "We lost our stabilizers.

I can't hold the ship steady!"

Red warning lights flashed and alarms sounded throughout the ship as Obi-Wan drew his lightsaber and closed in on General Grievous. The docking tube that connected the ships broke loose. All the air in the tube was quickly being sucked out. Cody grabbed Obi-Wan and pulled him to safety as several clones flew out of the tube and into open space.

General Grievous climbed into his ship and turned to look back at Obi-Wan. "Until we meet again, Kenobi!" he laughed.

But before Grievous could close the hatch, Adi Gallia appeared behind him. As she moved in with her lightsaber, the Republic ship below them exploded.

Adi Gallia was knocked down into the tube, but she grabbed onto the edge and pulled herself back into the ship. She quickly fired her ascension cable into the tube, allowing Cody and Obi-Wan to climb out.

They made their way up the docking tube and into Grievous's ship. Grievous was already gone, but at least Obi-Wan, Adi Gallia and Cody were safe. They closed the hatch behind them.

Obi-Wan pulled out his comlink and tried to reach Anakin. He knew that Anakin was their only chance of escape.

"Anakin, come in!" he said. "We're in a bit of a spot and we need a way off Grievous's ship."

Anakin responded quickly, his voice reassuring his friends. "There's a large hangar near your position. Make your way there and I'll pick you up."

General Grievous rocketed away in his escape pod toward his droid base on the planet Saleucami below. He knew that his ship was about to explode, and he hoped it would take the Jedi and their clones with it.

The Jedi and Commander Cody made their way to the hangar. As promised, Anakin was waiting for them. As soon as everyone was safely aboard Anakin's shuttle, they took off to join the Republic fleet.

They watched from the shuttle as the ship exploded and Grievous's escape pod headed for Saleucami. Obi-Wan and Anakin knew they had to go after him, but they would need to bring an army of ships and clone troopers with them if they wanted to stop him.

In the hangar bay of a Jedi cruiser, Anakin's shuttle landed safely. The Jedi helped bring Master Koth out of the small ship.

"Several crafts detached from Grievous's ship," Admiral Yularen reported over the comlink, "and attempted to land on Saleucami."

"We'll have to land and follow them," Obi-Wan replied. "Prepare the tanks."

"Yes, sir," Yularen said as he ended the communication.

Anakin looked at his former Master. "There must be several landing sites," he said. "It may be hard to locate the good general."

"You'll have to command the space battle," Obi-Wan said to Anakin, "while Rex, Cody and I head to the surface."

Obi-Wan had to act quickly. He knew that if he didn't get to the surface and find Grievous, the general would escape and the mission would be for nothing.

"Are you sure you can handle this on your own?" Anakin asked.

"I'm sure I can manage," Obi-Wan replied.

On the plant Saleucami, General Grievous stood by his crashed escape pod and stared into the sky. He knew that Obi-Wan and the Republic wouldn't be far behind.

"We must find a way off this planet before they find us," Grievous said to his droids as he spotted a Republic ship making its way past them. "We need to hurry."

"Contact the fleet," Grievous added.

"Sir, our transmitter is destroyed," a battle droid replied. "There is only one escape pod that survived."

Grievous growled. "We must get there as quickly as possible. Let's hope the transmitter is still intact."

The general surveyed the landscape and then ordered "Now find me some transportation."

The Republic transport landed several miles away from Grievous.
Immediately, the clone troopers began unloading AT-TEs and speeder bikes.

Obi-Wan decided that it would be best to head to the wreckage of
Grievous's ship first.

"Any sign of him?" Rex asked Obi-Wan as he pulled his speeder bike
alongside the Jedi who rode on the back of an AT-TE.

Obi-Wan looked down from his macrobinoculars and replied "I believe we've
found his ship."

At the crash site, the clone troopers began digging through the wreckage.
They were looking for clues to Grievous's location.

"These droids are too gone to give us any intel," a trooper said as he picked through the remains of destroyed battle droids.

Then a clone trooper spotted something. "Here's one," he shouted.

"Let's load the droid into the tank," Obi-Wan said after inspecting it. "We'll have a closer look at it on the go."

Inside the AT-TE, Cody and his men accessed the disabled droid's memory logs.

"According to its memory logs, Grievous fired the thrusters on the escape pod to avoid a mid-air collision," Cody reported to Obi-Wan.

"A collision with what?" Obi-Wan asked.

"Another pod," Clone Trooper Crys replied.

"Can you pinpoint the landing zone for the other pod?" Obi-Wan asked.

"I can put us within two or three clicks of it, sir," replied Cody.

"Alert the men," Obi-Wan ordered. "We've picked up the scent."

"There's our escape pod," Obi-Wan said as they approached the other crash site, signalling for his AT-TE to stop. "Any sign of Grievous?"

"It looks deserted," Cody replied as he looked through his macrobinoculars.

"He must be heading to a second escape pod," Obi-Wan added before activating the comlink on his wrist.

"Grievous is on the move," Obi-Wan told a team of clones on speeder bikes.

"We're headed to the west. Swing around and we can meet up at the second escape pod. We're going to need all the firepower we can muster."

"Is your transmitter working?" Grievous called to a battle droid at the landing site of the second escape pod.

"I don't know, I haven't used it yet," the droid replied.

Grievous angrily smashed the droid and sent it flying. "All right, I'll check on it," the droid said.

"Stupid battle droids," the general muttered as a second droid came out of the pod.

"You made it Sir," it called out.

"Get back into that pod and send out a distress signal towards the rest of the fleet. We need to get a shuttle down here immediately," Grievous ordered.

"Roger, roger," the droid replied. "But I must inform you sir, there are multiple life-forms approaching from the east and west."

"Ahhhhh! Battle positions!" Grievous growled.

The battle droid launched a missile towards the approaching AT-TE. Obi-Wan leaped from the tank just in time. The missile exploded, tearing the AT-TE apart.

A clone trooper yelled into his comlink. "Tank two! Port side!"

The tank swung its gun around and blasted the oncoming missile.

"Great shot!" the trooper added.

Grievous stood by, watching. "Where is that ship?!" he yelled.

"Finally!" Grievous growled as a Separatist shuttle arrived.

"General Grievous, sir," the droid pilot spoke into the shuttle's comlink, "we see you below us. Are you ready to depart?"

From the battle, Obi-Wan saw the shuttle approaching.

"Concentrate your fire on that ship," he ordered the AT-TEs. "Don't let it land."

"Cover me Cody," Obi-Wan called out as he charged towards Grievous. Grievous spun around and blocked the Jedi's lightsaber with his own.

Obi-Wan countered and knocked Grievous back.

The general flung his cape towards Obi-Wan and moved forward with two lightsabers spinning.

The Jedi drove Grievous back and trapped him against the side of the escape pod. Meanwhile, the Separatist shuttle pulled overhead.

"Forget trying to land," Grievous ordered into his comlink as he climbed up the side of the escape pod.

From the ground, Obi-Wan looked up and saw Grievous standing atop the pod. The shuttle moved in above him.

Obi-Wan quickly made his way up the side of the pod and after Grievous.

But before he could make it to the top, Grievous raised one arm and shot out a cable, which attached to the shuttle. "Fire the engines," Grievous ordered the shuttle pilot.

Obi-Wan reached out, hoping to grab the general. It was too late. Grievous was being lifted into the air.

The clone troopers fired at him, but he blocked their blasts with his lightsaber.

"Ha, ha, Jedi scum!" Grievous laughed as he was lifted to safety.

Obi-Wan sat on the escape pod, frustrated. "We're back to where we started," he said to Commander Cody.

General Grievous had escaped. Again.